Spellbound

Tales of Enchantment from Ancient Ireland

To my colleagues, Nessa and Elaina – *S.P.*
For my mother with love – *O.W.*

JANETTA OTTER-BARRY BOOKS

First published in Great Britain in 2012 and in the USA in 2013 by
Frances Lincoln Children's Books, 4 Torriano Mews,
Torriano Avenue, London NW5 2RZ
www.franceslincoln.com

A catalogue record for this book is available from the British Library.

ISBN 978-1-84780-140-1

Illustrated with watercolours

Set in Centaur MT

Printed in Shenzhen, Guangdong, China by C&C Offset Printing in July, 2012

1 3 5 7 9 8 6 4 2

Spellbound

Tales of Enchantment
from Ancient Ireland

Retold by
Siobhán Parkinson

Illustrated by
Olwyn Whelan

F
FRANCES LINCOLN
CHILDREN'S BOOKS

Contents

❧ Butterfly Girl ❧

A long time ago in Ireland, there lived a beautiful princess whose name was Etain. She was so beautiful that when she went walking, the birds of the air stopped singing to stare at her, the wind stopped sighing through the treetops and all the animals held their breath.

Her clear and lovely cheeks were as soft and smooth and red as foxglove petals. Her eyebrows were as black as a beetle's wing, and her teeth were like a shower of pearls. Her eyes were hyacinth blue and her lips were red. Her limbs were straight and soft and smooth. Her skin was as pale as sea-foam and her hands as white as a dusting of snowfall.

A chieftain called Midir fell in love with Etain the Beautiful, and before long the couple were married. But when Etain arrived as a bride at Midir's castle, she discovered that her new husband was married already.

Midir's first wife was not happy at all. In fact, she was so angry and jealous that she decided to get rid of Etain. So she cast a magic spell and turned the beautiful young girl into a butterfly. Then she left Midir's house and went back to her own family.

Poor Etain! She could not walk or talk or eat proper food or sleep in a bed or do anything that people do. She now had to live her life as a butterfly.

But she was just as beautiful as a butterfly as she had been when she was a princess. Her shimmering wings were the most exquisite shades

of mauve and violet and pink and crimson, and her eyes shone like precious jewels.

She could not speak, but she could sing, and her voice was sweeter than the music of the sweetest harp. Everywhere she flew, she made people happy. Sick people got better and hungry people felt full, and everyone danced and sang for sheer delight.

Only Midir was sad, because he had lost his beautiful young wife. But everywhere he went, the butterfly Etain flew along beside him and sang sweet songs to cheer him up. At night, when he lay down to sleep, she fluttered round his head and flapped her wings gently, so that he nodded off to the soft humming of her crimson wings. Gradually he got used to having a gorgeous butterfly as his companion instead of his lovely wife.

Now, Midir's first wife heard that Midir and Etain were still together, even though Etain was a butterfly.

"This won't do!" she muttered. "I have to find another way to get rid of Etain." So she thought up a wicked plan. She closed her eyes and waved her arms and cast a new spell. "Blow, wind!" she cried.

Suddenly a great gust of wind came roaring in from the sea. The leaves were stripped from the trees, the grass was snatched out of the earth, and the waves of the sea came crashing towards the shore. The people all ran indoors and closed their windows, and waited for the storm to pass. But the poor little butterfly Etain had not the strength in her gorgeous wings to fly away from the storm. She was blown about and whirled around, and finally she was whisked right out to sea.

Etain was carried so far out to sea by the storm that for seven long years the poor little butterfly could not find her way home. All day long she flew over the waves, desperately searching for land. And at night, the only places she could find to rest were rocks and deserted islands in the middle of the ocean.

After seven desperate years at sea, Etain finally managed to find her way back to Ireland. As soon as she landed and had rested her weary wings, she set off to look for Midir. But she had no idea what part of the country she was in, or where to begin to look for Midir's castle.

She flew up to the top of a tree, to see if she could spot anything that would give her a clue, but all she could see were rocks and stones and grassy pathways that she could not recognise. It was no use, she thought. She would never find Midir.

Just then, she spied a young man she knew. His name was Aengus, and he was a relation of Midir's. She fluttered down from her treetop and alighted on Aengus's shoulder.

Now, Aengus knew that Etain had been turned into a butterfly and whooshed out to sea by Midir's first wife all those years ago. And although Etain could not speak to him, he recognised her at once.

"Good morning, Etain!" he said to the pretty little butterfly who was perched on the shoulder of his cloak. "You are welcome home to Ireland."

Etain gave a joyful little flap of her wings.

Aengus took the butterfly Etain home with him. He made a little house for her, with windows, so that she could fly in and out. Everywhere he went, he carried the butterfly house with him, so that he could look after Etain and make sure she was all right.

All was well for a while, but then Midir's first wife got to hear that Etain had arrived back in Ireland. She grew very angry again. She closed her eyes and waved her arms and cast another magic spell. She blew up another powerful wind, and poor little Etain was driven out to sea again.

When Aengus found that the little butterfly house was empty, he knew perfectly well who was to blame. He stormed off to Midir's first wife's house, and when she came out to see who was knocking on the door, Aengus cut her head right off with one swift swipe of his sword.

"At least Etain will be safe now," he said as he mounted his horse. Then he galloped away, leaving the headless body of the evil woman bleeding on the ground.

Poor Etain was still out at sea, being blown about by the wind, just as before. After many years, she managed to find her way back to Ireland again, and this time she flew into a banqueting hall and landed, splash, in a glass of wine. The wine glass belonged to the wife of a chieftain called Étar. Étar's wife was chattering merrily to the person next to her, and she never noticed that a pretty little butterfly had landed, splash, in her wine. Without looking into her glass, she drank the wine and swallowed the butterfly Etain along with it.

You might think that was the end of poor little Etain – but it wasn't. The butterfly flew right down into the woman's body and found a nice warm spot, where she settled down and went into a deep sleep.

Some months later, Étar's wife gave birth to a baby girl. And... have you guessed it? This new baby was really Etain. She wasn't a butterfly any more, but had changed into a human baby girl.

The baby did not remember anything about her life as a butterfly, or her life before that as the wife of Midir. She was just a normal baby, who needed to be fed and looked after by her parents and to grow up and learn about the world.

Étar and his wife named their new baby Etain, and the new Etain grew up to be just as beautiful as the first one.

Now, just as the new Etain was growing into a young woman, the High King of Ireland was looking for a wife. He sent his men out to find a suitable girl for him to marry. The king's men rode up and down the country, riding the length and breadth of Ireland in search of a wife for the king. They rode over and back across the land, and they met many lovely young girls, but it was not until they found Etain, daughter of Étar, that they knew they had discovered the right young woman for the king.

The king's men went back to the royal palace and told the king about the beautiful girl they had found. They told him where she lived, and they said that he should go and take a look for himself.

So the king went out looking for this beautiful young girl, Etain. He followed the directions his men had given him, and one day he found her. She had come to a well to wash her hair. He knew it must be Etain, because she was so beautiful.

She was wearing a rich crimson cloak fastened with a brooch of silver and gold. The king moved his horse behind a tree and he watched as she lowered the hood of her cloak.

Her clear and lovely cheeks were as soft and smooth and red as foxglove petals. Her eyebrows were as black as a beetle's wing, and her teeth were like a shower of pearls. Her eyes were hyacinth blue and her lips were red. Her limbs were straight and soft and smooth. Her skin was as pale as sea foam and her hands as white as a dusting of snowfall.

She wore a comb of silver and gold in her glorious hair. When she loosened her hair from its comb, it bloomed like a flower. She washed her hair in a basin of silver with four gold birds engraved on it, and it was bright with tiny crimson gems.

The king straightaway fell in love with this beautiful girl. He came out from behind the tree and spoke to the lovely young woman, and it was not long before they were married.

But the High King was not the only man to love Etain. In the king's army was a man called Ailill, and this Ailill fell so badly in love with Etain that he thought he would die of love for her. Gentle Etain got to hear that poor Ailill was very unhappy, and she agreed that she would meet him one evening and try to cheer him up. Now you will remember that in her past life Etain had been married to a man called Midir. Midir got to hear that Etain was back in Ireland, that she was married now to the High King, and that she had arranged to meet the lovesick Ailill.

Midir was overcome with jealousy. He cast a spell on Ailill, which made him fall fast asleep, and so he missed his appointment to meet Etain. Then, while Ailill was sleeping, Midir put on Ailill's cloak and took Ailill's sword and shield, and set off to meet Etain in Ailill's place.

When Etain met 'Ailill' (who was really Midir), he told her the whole story. "Etain," he said, "I know you are just a young girl, but I have to tell you that in another life you were a butterfly."

Etain was astonished to hear this strange news.

"And before that," said Midir, "you were my wife."

"But..." started Etain, still amazed.

"A wicked woman who was jealous of our happy marriage turned you into a butterfly, and then later you were reborn as the very same girl you used to be."

Etain shook her head. This could not be true. She was the wife of the High King, not of this strange man.

"All these years, Etain, I have been searching for you, and now I have found you, you must come back with me to my castle and live there with me as my loving wife."

"But I am married to the king," said Etain, "and he is a good man. I cannot just leave him and go with you."

"But you are really my wife, not his."

Etain thought about this for a while. She wanted to be fair to Midir, but she did not want to leave her husband. In the end, she said, "Well, Midir, if you can persuade my husband the king to let you

kiss me, then I will know that he does not love me as much as you do, and I will go with you."

So the next day, Midir went to the king and challenged him to a game of chess.

"I bet you fifty horses that I can beat you," he announced. "Fifty of my finest steeds, grey and black and white, and all with silver manes."

The king loved to play chess, and he loved it even more if there was a good prize to play for, so he readily agreed. Midir came to the king's castle the following evening, and they played and played, until long past midnight.

Midir was a champion chess player, but he was too clever to win this game against the king. After many hours of play, he made a bad move, and the king pounced and won the game.

"Ah, you are the better player!" said Midir, and he stood up to go home. "I will send the horses at first light tomorrow morning. And tomorrow night, we will play again?"

The king was delighted to have won, and he eagerly agreed to another match.

Every night for a month, Midir and the king played chess, and every night, Midir made sure the king won the game.

The king won silver and gold from Midir, rings and jewels and swords and shields, tapestries and blankets and furnishings, and fine copper pots and oak chests inlaid with precious metals and full of delicious foods, herds of cattle and tracts of land, bolts of silken cloth and embroidered cloaks, and precious stones and barrels of wine and fine leathers and skins and wools.

Midir handed over all the winnings without a murmur.

In the end, Midir said he was going to have to give up playing chess with the king.

"I can't go on playing you," he said. "Every time we play, I lose more of my riches. If I go on like this, I will be a poor man."

But by now the king had got used to winning, and he wanted to go on winning. "One last game," he said, "and you can name your own prize."

16

Midir pretended to think long and hard about this offer and, in the end, he agreed.

The next evening, Midir came to the royal castle and, as usual, the two men played late into the night. But what was not usual was that this time Midir planned to win.

"Checkmate!" he cried at last, and the game ended.

"You won!" said the king, astounded.

"Yes," said Midir, trying to sound surprised. "I suppose my luck has changed."

"And what would you like as your prize?" asked the king. "I can give you fifty fine horses, for example, grey ones and black ones and white ones, and all with silver manes."

"No, thank you," said Midir. "I have plenty of horses."

"Jewels?" said the king. "Silk? Oak chests? Rugs?"

"No," said Midir. "What I would like is a kiss from your wife, Etain the Beautiful."

"You want to kiss my wife?" stormed the king. "That is outrageous! I will not hear of it."

"You said I could name my prize," said Midir quietly. "If you go back on your word now, no one will ever believe you again when you make a bargain."

And so the king had to agree. His honour was at stake.

When Midir came to the castle the next evening to claim his kiss, Etain was in the banqueting hall, serving wine. Her clear and lovely cheeks were as soft and smooth and red as foxglove petals. Her eyebrows were as black... well, you know the rest.

The king watched as Midir strode through the banqueting hall and walked right up to Etain, put his arms round her and kissed her.

And then an amazing thing happened. As Midir and Etain kissed, their cloaks and garments fell away to reveal beautiful white feathers covering their bodies. Right in front of the king and his courtiers, Midir and Etain turned into white swans and, with their graceful necks entwined, they flapped their wings softly and flew into the air, up through the chimney and right up, up into the sky.

Away they flew, the pair of them, up through the clouds, and all that was left in the banqueting hall was their human clothing, shining brightly on the floor near the fireplace. And overhead the people could hear the steady swish, swish, swish of swans' wings, as Etain and Midir flew away, together at last.

The Enchanted Deer

Fionn Mac Cumhaill was the leader of the great band of warriors of ancient Ireland known as the Fianna.

The men of the Fianna were brave and strong. They were so fleet and light of foot that they could run through the forest without breaking so much as a single twig, and yet they were strong in body and quick with the sword. They were famous not only for their strength and speed and bravery, but for their sense of fairness. They were kind to poor people and old people and people who were sick or sad or in need of help.

One day when Fionn was out hunting in the forest, his dogs ran wildly ahead of him, yapping with excitement. Fionn followed the sound of their delirious barking, and their voices led him into a clearing. The dogs were leaping and barking at a beautiful white doe, who was trapped in a thorny hedge and could not move.

Fionn saw the trapped animal, and thought what a fine feast he and his warriors would have when they killed it. He raised his bow to shoot the deer, but before he could let the arrow fly, the animal spoke to him in a human voice.

"Don't shoot!" she begged. "Please don't kill me."

Fionn was so astonished that he lowered his bow, and instead of shooting the deer, he freed her from the thorns that trapped her. Then he led her out of the clearing in the forest and took her back to his castle.

As they made their way home to Fionn's castle, the doe spoke to him. "Thank you for sparing my life," she said in a gentle voice.

"Who are you?" asked Fionn. "For I know you cannot really be a deer."

"You are right," said the deer. "My name is Sadhbh, and I am the daughter of a chieftain. A wicked witch put me under an evil spell, and now I have to live my daytime life as a deer in the forest."

Fionn found her story hard to believe, but after all, how else would a deer be able to talk?

When they arrived at the castle, Fionn took the deer inside, and at first she lay down gratefully in front of the fire. But when dusk started to fall, the deer grew restless. She stood up from the hearth and started to move about.

"I'm thirsty," she said, and Fionn went out to get her a drink.

When he came back with the water, he was astonished to see not a white doe but a beautiful young woman standing on the floor in front of his fire. She was wearing the fine silken clothing of a wealthy woman, and her golden hair rippled over her shoulders and down her back, like a glorious curtain of cloth-of-gold. She put out a lily-white hand, and Fionn dipped a goblet in the pail of water he was carrying and handed it to her.

"Sadhbh?" he asked, as she sipped the water with lips as red as holly berries.

"Yes," said the lovely young woman. "I live as a deer by day, as you have seen, but at nightfall I turn back into human form."

Fionn fell instantly in love with Sadhbh, and she with him, and they lived together very happily for a long time. During the day, Sadhbh would take on the form of a beautiful white doe and go roaming about Fionn's fields and forests, and at night she would come home in the form of a beautiful young woman, and have supper with Fionn, and sleep in the castle.

One day, Fionn had to go away on a long trip.

"I will be gone for some time," he told Sadhbh, "but I promise I will return. Will you wait for me?"

Sadhbh agreed that she would wait, but after many weeks and months, she grew lonely and restless. At last, she could stand it no longer, and she wandered away from the castle and went back into the woods, and was never seen again.

Fionn was broken-hearted when he came home from his journey to find that Sadhbh had left him. He gathered his dogs and his men together and they all rode out into the forest to see if they could find the magic white doe again.

Fionn never did find Sadhbh, but instead he found a beautiful young boy sitting under a tree. He was naked except for his long golden hair, and he told Fionn that his mother was a deer, and that his name was Oisín, which means 'little deer'.

When Fionn heard this, he knew at once that Oisín was the son of the deer-woman Sadhbh, and his own son also. So he leaned down from his horse and swept the little boy up into his arms. He put him in front

of him on his saddle and together they rode home to Fionn's castle.

Fionn brought Oisín up as the son of a Fianna warrior, and trained him to shoot with his bow and arrow, fight with his sword and protect himself with his shield. He taught him to run and jump and leap, and to skim through the forest so swiftly and lightly that he never broke so much as a twig.

When Oisín grew up, he joined the Fianna and became his father's right-hand man and one of the greatest warriors in the land. But sight nor sound there never was again of Sadhbh, the beautiful enchanted deer.

 # Land Under Wave

One snowy night, an ugly bedraggled old hag came knocking on the door of a house where some of the men of the Fianna were lodged for the night.

The men of the Fianna opened the door to the old hag, but they were not very pleased to see her, for she was ugly and wrinkled. Her hair was matted and tangled, her clothes were dirty and torn, and she did not smell too good either. However, it was a very cold night, so they let her in.

The bedraggled old hag put out a hand that was stiff and gnarled, with blackened fingernails, and tugged at Fionn's blanket.

"I am cold," she said. "May I share your blanket tonight, sir?"

But Fionn shrank back from the wretched creature and refused.

Next she turned to Oisín, son of Fionn, and asked him the same question.

But like his father, Oisín was repelled by the horrible old creature with her cold and smelly feet and her wrinkled, warty skin, and he too refused.

25

Finally, she asked Diarmaid, one of the other men of the Fianna, if she might sleep under his blanket.

"Well," said Diarmaid, "you are an awful-looking old creature, but the men of the Fianna are pledged to be kind to people who are old and weak and in distress. I can see that you are cold, so, all right, you can share my blanket."

The ugly old hag lay down beside Diarmaid, and instantly she turned into a beautiful young woman. All the men were astounded by her beauty, and they were sorry now that they had been so harsh to her.

The beautiful young woman and Diarmaid fell instantly in love, and within a few days, they had married and set up house together.

The young woman made Diarmaid promise one thing, and this was it: "Do not remind me three times about how terrible I looked when you first met me."

Well, Diarmaid did not want to remind her even once about how horrible she had looked when she was an old hag, so he willingly agreed that he would never mention it.

Time passed, and one day Diarmaid needed to leave his beautiful wife and go away on some Fianna business. But he didn't want to go, because his favourite greyhound had just had a litter of three lovely black and brown puppies, and he would have liked to stay and look after them.

"Don't worry about the dogs," said his wife. "You go about your business, and I will see to them."

So Diarmaid left the pups and their mother to the care of his wife, and away he went.

Now, while Diarmaid was away, Fionn came riding by the house, and the young wife invited him in for a drink.

"What fine pups you have there," said Fionn, when he caught sight of the basket of puppies and their mother.

"Yes," said the young wife. "Diarmaid has left me in charge of them.

Would you like to have one for yourself?"

Fionn was delighted. He chose his favourite puppy, a lovely, lively bundle of mischief, and off he went with the pup wrapped warmly under his cloak.

When Diarmaid came home that evening, he was very angry to see that his pup had been given away.

He shouted at his wife. "Who do you think you are that you can be giving my dogs away? You were only a horrible old hag when I first saw you, and you still would be if I hadn't been kind to you. And this is the thanks I get!"

The woman said, "You promised you would not remind me of that," and Diarmaid had to admit that he had made that promise. So he apologised to his wife and they made up their quarrel.

The next day, Diarmaid had to go away again, and this time Oisín came riding by the house. Again the wife gave Oisín a present of one of the pups, and Oisín went away very pleased with himself.

When Diarmaid came home and found the second pup had been

given away, he lost his temper, and once more he shouted at his wife. "Who do you think you are that you can be giving my dogs away? You were only a horrible old hag when I first saw you, and you still would be if I hadn't been kind to you. And this is the thanks I get!"

Once more she reproached him for mentioning how she had looked when he first met her, and again he apologised, and they made it up.

On the third day that Diarmaid had to go away, another man of the Fianna came by, and the woman gave away the last pup of the litter.

This time, Diarmaid was in a howling rage. For a third time he insulted his wife. "Who do you think you are that you can be giving my dogs away? You were only a horrible old hag when I first saw you, and you still would be if I hadn't been kind to you. And this is the thanks I get! I wish I had never laid eyes on you!"

Now he had really gone too far.

"You swore to me," she said, "that you would not remind me three times of how I looked when we met, and now you have done exactly what you promised you would not do. You have insulted me three times."

Again Diarmaid remembered his promise and he opened his mouth to apologise for a third time, but it was too late. His house suddenly disappeared in front of his eyes, and his beautiful young wife with it.

So Diarmaid set off to look for his lady. He walked and walked and he found his greyhound, mother of all the pups that had been given away, lying dead on the road in a pool of blood. He was very sad to see the poor dog in such a pitiable state.

Diarmaid went on walking, and he came across a drop of blood on the path. He thought it must be from the poor greyhound, so he wiped it up with his handkerchief and went on. After a little while, he found another spot of blood on the road in front of him, and again he wiped it up. And a third time he found a drop of blood and used his handkerchief to mop it up.

Still there was no sign of Diarmaid's wife, and as he went along, he asked the people he met on the road if they had seen her going that way. Some of them said yes, they had seen a beautiful young woman on the road, so Diarmaid kept on walking. And at last he came to the golden strand, where the sea washed ceaselessly against the shore.

He found a boat lying on the sands, so he got into it, raised the sail, and off he sailed over the waves. Days passed and nights

30

passed and Diarmaid was growing tired and hungry and his limbs were stiff with cold and salt. But still there was no sign of land, and there was certainly no sign of his lovely young wife.

After sailing very far from Ireland, the boat suddenly started to sink. Down it went, down under the water to the sea-bed, and down went Diarmaid with it.

At last the boat landed on the sea-bed, and Diarmaid stepped out. He found that he could breathe down here, and that his clothes did not get wet. So he started to walk along the plain under the sea.

As he walked, he saw a woman cutting rushes. He stopped and asked her where he was.

"Good day to you, sir," she said, straightening up from her work. "This is Land Under Wave."

Diarmaid asked the woman why she was cutting the rushes.

"I am cutting them for the princess," said the woman. "The king's daughter has been away for a long time, and she has only recently returned. But now she is sick, very sick, and the only thing that makes her comfortable is a fine soft bed of rushes."

When Diarmaid heard that the princess had been away from home for a long time, he knew at once who this princess was. "Your princess — I must see her. I am sure I can make her well again."

The woman looked at him doubtfully, but no one else had been able to do anything for the poor sick princess, so she thought that maybe it was worth giving this young warrior a chance.

"Take me to her," Diarmaid pleaded.

"Nobody is allowed to see her," said the rush-cutter. "She is too ill for visitors."

"Well, then," said Diarmaid, "smuggle me in. Hide me in your rushes."

So the woman made a bundle of rushes and put them under Diarmaid and over him, so that he was well hidden. Then she threw the bundle over her shoulder and went to the castle of the King of Land Under Wave.

The guards let the old woman with her bundle of rushes into the princess's bedroom, and she threw her heavy bundle on to the floor.

The princess watched as the bundle of rushes started to move, and Diarmaid came rolling out. She was amazed and delighted to see him, and she put out a thin, pale hand to greet him.

"What has made you so sick?" asked Diarmaid, grief-stricken.

"I cut myself very badly on thorns and brambles on my journey home," she said. "I lost a lot of blood, and now I am weak."

"Is there no cure?" asked Diarmaid anxiously, kissing her poor thin hand.

"I need to get back the blood I lost," said the princess. "But how can I do that?"

Then Diarmaid produced his handkerchief, and it was soaked in the blood of the princess.

"That is wonderful," she said, hope brightening her eyes, "but I must drink it from the cup of healing."

"What is that?'" asked Diarmaid.

"It's a special goblet that belongs to the King of the Plain of Wonder."

"Tell me where to go, and I will bring it to you," said Diarmaid.

The princess gave him directions, and so Diarmaid kissed her goodbye and set out to find the Plain of Wonder.

He soon came to a river, as the princess had said he would, which marked the boundary between the Land Under Wave and the Plain of Wonder. But there was no boat, and Diarmaid did not know how he would get across.

But then a little red man appeared. He put out his hand and cupped Diarmaid's foot in his palm. And in this way, the little man brought Diarmaid safely across the river.

When Diarmaid arrived at the house of the King of the Plain of Wonder, an army of fighting men came out to defend the palace. But Diarmaid took out his sword and swung it over his head. He charged at the men and killed every last one of them.

The king was astonished by a man who could defeat a whole army single-handed, and he asked him to name his prize. Diarmaid replied that he wanted the healing cup, and so impressed by his strength and skill was the king that he handed the cup to Diarmaid without a murmur.

Diarmaid took the cup and set off back to the river, and the little red man appeared again and brought him safely to the opposite bank. When they arrived back in Land Under Wave, the little red man told Diarmaid that he should mix the blood with water from a magic well, and give it to his wife in the healing cup, and this would make her better.

"But," he warned, "there is a snag. When she drinks it, your love for her will disappear like the morning dew."

Diarmaid did not believe that his love for the beautiful princess would ever fade, so he took the water from the well the little red man had pointed out to him, and he mixed it with the blood from his handkerchief in the healing cup.

This time, he did not need to hide in a bundle of rushes. He went up to the guards outside the princess's room. "I have the potion that will cure the king's daughter," he told them. "Her own blood, mixed with water from the magic well and served in the healing cup given to me by the King of the Plain of Wonder."

The princess was even weaker now, but when she saw Diarmaid with the cup of healing in his hands, she smiled and took the drink from him and put it to her lips.

With every sip she took, she grew stronger. The colour came back into her cheeks, and her hair started to look strong and shiny.

Diarmaid's heart was glad to see his young wife getting better before his eyes. But as she drained the last drops from the cup, his love for her suddenly disappeared like a puff of smoke, and he remembered what the little red man had foretold.

The princess knew at once what had happened, for she felt Diarmaid's love draining away from her, even as her strength came back. They were both sad that their love had died, but they agreed that there was nothing they could do about it. They would just have to part.

And so the King of Land Under Wave gave Diarmaid a fine ship to sail home to Ireland in, and he went away, back to his friends in the Fianna. He never saw his lovely princess again, but all his life he never forgot her.

The Children of Lir

Once there was a king in Ireland called Lir.

Lir's wife had died, leaving him with four children — three fine sons and a beautiful daughter called Fionnuala. Lir and his children loved each other, and although they were sad about the death of Lir's wife, they were happy together. But as his children were growing up, Lir thought it would be better for them to have a mother as well as a father, and so he married a new wife.

Lir's new wife's name was Aoife.

At first everything was fine. Aoife loved Lir, and she loved his four children; she was a good mother to them, and they were a happy family. But as time went on and Aoife saw how much Lir loved his children, she began to think that he had not married her for herself, but only so that she would be a mother for his children.

She began to feel jealous of the children, and she wished they were not there, so that she could have Lir all to herself. And so she came up with a wicked plan to get rid of them.

One summer's day, when Lir was away from home, Aoife suggested to the children that they should go to the lake for a swim. The children were hot, and the thought of a swim in the cool waters of the lake was delicious. They all got into the chariot with Aoife, and off they sped to the shores of the lake.

The lake sparkled grey and cool under the high, blue summer sky, and all around the edges were smooth grey stones and soft green weeds. It all looked very inviting under the burning summer sun, and the children couldn't wait to get out of their tunics and trousers and jump gleefully into the lovely fresh water. Aoife remained on the shore, to look after their clothes.

Nobody knew it, but Aoife was secretly training to be a witch, and already she had evil powers. As the children were swimming and splashing about in the cool water, Aoife stood on the lake's edge. She spread

her arms out over their swimming bodies and started to work a terrible spell.

Just then, Lir came riding by, on his way home, and he heard the voices of the children laughing and shouting from the water. He stopped to look, but imagine his astonishment when he saw not his four lovely children but four beautiful swans splashing and shouting in the lake water. He ran up to Aoife and grabbed her by the arms.

"What have you done, Aoife?" shouted Lir, dropping to the ground in his grief. "Turn them back into children, I beg of you."

Aoife was sorry when she saw how grief-stricken her husband was, but she was not a powerful enough witch to undo her spell.

"I cannot," she said. "I don't know the antidote to the spell. All I can do is stop now, before they lose their human voices. They must remain as swans for nine hundred years. They will spend three hundred years on this lake, then three hundred years on the River Moyle and the last three hundred years they must spend on Lake Derravaragh."

"Nine hundred years!" wailed Lir. "My poor, poor children!"

The only consolation Lir had was that the children still had the power of human speech, and were able to talk to each other.

"In nine hundred years, they will turn back into humans," said Aoife, "at the sound of the church bell."

Nobody knew what she meant, for nobody had ever heard of a church, since this all happened in the time before Christianity came to Ireland.

Lir immediately divorced his wicked wife and sent her away. After that, he came every day to the lakeside to visit his children. The swans would swim up to him and he would sit on the edge of the lake, gather them around him and they would talk and sing and tell stories.

This went on for many years, until eventually Lir died, and then the swan children were all alone on the cold lake. As their stepmother had predicted, they spent three hundred years there, and then three hundred miserable years on the River Moyle and a final cold three hundred years on Lake Derravaragh.

All this long and wretched time, Fionnuala looked after her brothers, and every night they would sleep huddled together under her protecting wings.

One day, at the end of nine hundred years, the ringing tones of a large metal bell pealed out over the waters of Lake Derravaragh.

The swan children had never heard a sound like this before, but they remembered what Aoife had said about something called a church bell, and they realised that the spell was coming to an end.

In a flurry of excitement, they swam to the shore, and as they stood at the water's edge, their feathers fell away and their large orange webbed feet turned into human feet with toes.

But the children's feet were old and gnarled, and their beautiful swans' wings gave way to grey and wasted human limbs. Of course, they were no longer children. They were over nine hundred years old.

The four old children of Lir were glad to be human again, but the land that they now walked was completely unfamiliar to them. Their father and everyone they had loved was dead, and they knew that it was time for them to die too. And when they did die, the people buried them together in the churchyard. They laid the three old men side by side in three graves, and Fionnuala's grave across the heads of her brothers' graves, so that she could still embrace them all in death, and protect them as she had in life.

The Enchanted Birds

King Conor Mac Nessa of Ulster had a sister called Dechtire. Princess Dechtire was getting married to a man called Sualtim, and there was a great wedding feast at the royal castle. There were fifty beautiful bridesmaids in gorgeous gowns and jewels, and of course the loveliest of all was the bride, Princess Dechtire.

Everyone was very happy, except the great god Lugh of the Long Arm. Lugh didn't at all like the idea of Princess Dechtire getting married to Sualtim, because he wanted her for himself. So he thought up a secret plan.

There was a goblet of wine on the table in front of the bride at the wedding-feast, and when she wasn't looking, Lugh turned himself into a mayfly and flew right into Dechtire's wine goblet.

When Dechtire reached for her wine, she never noticed that there was an insect in it. She took a long drink, and she swallowed the mayfly without knowing a thing about it. The wine made Dechtire sleepy, so she called her fifty bridesmaids and they all went off to the women's part of the castle, so that Dechtire could have a little lie-down.

Dechtire did not know that Lugh of the Long Arm was actually inside her body, in the form of a mayfly, but while she was sleeping, Lugh appeared to Dechtire in her dreams, in human form.

"I love you, Dechtire," he whispered. "You belong to me now, not to Sualtim."

Dechtire woke up and looked around. She called for her maidens, but nobody came. She stood up from her bed and looked down to make sure her wedding gown was in order — but she wasn't wearing a wedding gown. She wasn't wearing any kind of gown. Her whole body was covered in feathers. She tried to put her hand to her face, but she had no hands, only wings.

Back at the wedding-feast, time was going by, and still the bride and her bridesmaids did not return from their rest. People began to wonder what had happened to them. Of course, they knew nothing about the way that Lugh of the Long Arm had enchanted Dechtire.

When Dechtire and her bridesmaids did not return to the feast, the wedding guests went looking for them. They searched high up and low down, all over the castle, but the bride and her bridesmaids were nowhere to be found.

The men came back to the banqueting hall without the young women. It seemed as if they had all disappeared into thin air. But when they looked out of the window, the people saw a beautiful flock of birds flying high up into the sky.

A great sadness fell upon the castle and upon the king, because they had lost all their beautiful young women and their lovely princess, and the people went into mourning.

Some months later, Dechtire's brother, Conor Mac Nessa, King of Ulster, was looking sadly out of the window of his castle when a beautiful flock of birds came swooping down on to his fields. The birds were linked together in pairs by tiny silver chains. Some of the pairs were more brightly coloured than the others and were linked by chains of gold.

The coloured pairs with the gold chains were each in charge of a little flock of silver-chained birds. They made a lovely sight as they came fluttering down and landed on the grass and started to graze.

The birds looked very beautiful, but soon the king realised that they were gobbling up all the grass. Pretty soon there was not so much as a single blade of grass left on the ground.

King Conor and his men were very angry when they saw their lush green grasslands being destroyed. They ran out of the castle and started to chase the birds.

The birds were startled, and they flew up into the air, their little chains gleaming and sparkling in the sunshine. The men got into their chariots and they sped along for many miles, chasing the birds away from the fields.

Eventually the birds disappeared from view, and night started to fall. King Conor and his friends were now a long way from home, and there was no sign of the birds. It was getting cold, and Conor and his men looked around, wondering where they might spend the night.

Then they spotted a large brightly lit house. If they were lucky, they thought, the people who lived there might give them a bed for the night. So they went up to the house and knocked. This beautiful house was in fact the palace of Brú na Bóinne, where the gods lived.

A tall handsome warrior in a shining suit of armour opened the door. He welcomed the men, and said that of course they could stay the night. So the men of Ulster went into the gorgeous palace – and who do you think they found there? It was the fifty bridesmaids who had disappeared from the wedding feast at the royal castle all that time ago!

The bridesmaids were delighted to see Conor and his men. "We were expecting you," they chirped, as they fluttered around, getting the bedrooms ready for the men. "In fact, we went to get you!"

For of course the beautiful flock of birds had really been the bridesmaids. They'd been turned into birds by Lugh of the Long Arm. As birds they had been spirited away from the castle. And as birds they had flown back to bring Conor and his men to their new home.

"Why did you want us to come here?" asked Conor.

"Dechtire wanted you to come," twittered the bridesmaids.

"But where is Dechtire now?" they asked, for there was no sign of her.

"She's in her own room," the bridesmaids said. "She is glad you are here, but she can't see you this evening. She is busy. In fact – she's having a baby!"

The next morning, Dechtire appeared, with her new baby son in her arms, and there was great rejoicing.

Conor Mac Nessa, King of Ulster, said, "Sister, please come back

home with us. We have all missed you. And your husband Sualtim has been heartbroken ever since you left on your wedding day."

Dechtire said, "Brother, I long to come home. That is why I sent for you. But this child is not my husband's son. His father is the god Lugh of the Long Arm. Will he be welcome at the royal castle?"

"Of course, Dechtire, you may bring your little boy with you. Sualtim will be so glad to see you, and we will bring up the baby in the royal family, where he belongs."

Dechtire was relieved to hear this. She wanted to get away from Lugh and she wanted to take her son back to Ulster. So they all climbed into the chariots, and sped home to Conor's castle.

Dechtire's husband was delighted to see his bride coming home and he welcomed the baby she brought with her. Dechtire and Sualtim named the boy Setanta and Sualtim raised him as his son. Nobody except Dechtire and Sualtim, and of course Conor Mac Nessa, knew that Setanta's father was really the great god Lugh of the Long Arm, who had stolen Dechtire away from her wedding feast.

Setanta grew up strong and handsome and was a favourite with everyone at the royal court. The king's wise man predicted that one day he would be a great warrior who would defend his people and be admired and loved by all.

And that is exactly what happened.

❧ Cú Chulainn and Emer ❧

Setanta was the son of Dechtire, sister of Conor Mac Nessa, King of Ulster.

While he was still a young boy, Setanta killed the guard dog of a man called Culann. To make up to Culann for killing his dog, Setanta stood guard outside Culann's castle, acting as a watchdog, while Culann was training up a new dog. Because of this, he was given the new name of Cú Chulainn, which means 'the hound of Culann'.

When he grew up, Setanta joined Conor Mac Nessa's special warrior band, who were known as the Knights of the Red Branch.

The young warrior Cú Chulainn fell in love with a beautiful young woman called Emer, and he wanted to marry her. But Emer's father, Forgall, was not happy about this, and he set about trying to get rid of Cú Chulainn.

He thought the best plan would be for Cú Chulainn to leave the country, so he went to the young man's parents, and told them they should send their son to Scotland, to be trained by the famous warrior and weapons-woman, Scatha. This would get the young man out of the way for a time, Forgall thought, and he would probably be killed on the journey, which was known to be very difficult and dangerous.

Cú Chulainn did not want to leave the lovely young Emer, but Emer herself thought he should go.

"If you are trained by Scatha," she said, "who is the finest javelin-thrower in the world, it would be a feather in your cap. There is a lot she could teach you about the use of swords and daggers and javelins, and you would come home a hero."

"And then would you marry me?" asked Cú Chulainn.

"Then I would marry you," said Emer with a smile.

And so it was that Cú Chulainn set out for Scotland. The journey was long and hard, and Cú Chulainn did not know the way.

He was quite lost when he spied a terrible lion-like beast coming towards him. It was a fierce-looking animal with a big shaggy head, and its enormous mouth was full of sharp fangs. But Cú Chulainn was not afraid, and sure enough, when the beast came up to him, it did not attack him, but greeted him like an old friend.

The beast went ahead of Cú Chulainn, as if to show him the way, and every now and again it would look back to make sure he was

following. Then it stopped altogether, and waited quietly for him. So Cú Chulainn leapt on to its back, and away they went. They journeyed for some days like this, and then the beast left Cú Chulainn, and he went on alone.

Next, Cú Chulainn met a young man, and he asked him the way to Scatha's house. The young man told him that he had a long journey ahead, and he would have to cross the Plain of Bad Luck.

"What kind of bad luck is in that place?" asked Cú Chulainn.

"There are two parts to this plain," the other lad told him. "The first half is impossible to cross, because your feet stick to the ground and you can't move."

"And the second part?" asked Cú Chulainn.

"Well," said the young fellow, "even if you did manage to cross the first part, things get even worse after that, because on the far side of the plain, every blade of grass is truly a blade, and all these blades spike through your feet and keep you nailed to the spot."

Cú Chulainn did not know how he would manage to cross this plain, but the young man gave him a wheel.

"It's a magic wheel," he said. "Follow the path the wheel makes through the first half of the plain, and you will be safe. Your feet will not stick to the ground." Then he also gave him an apple. "It's a magic apple," he told Cú Chulainn. "Throw the apple ahead of you and follow where it goes, and you will come safely out of the plain without your feet being pierced by the blades of grass."

Cú Chulainn did as he had been told, and he crossed the Plain of Bad Luck safely. After that, he came to a valley full of fearsome monsters,

sent there by Forgall to destroy him. They were much uglier than the friendly beast had been. They were all kinds of colours and some of them had two or three heads and some of them no heads at all.

But Cú Chulainn found a narrow path that went through the valley. He followed this path, and the monsters did not harm him.

Next, Cú Chulainn met a group of Scatha's pupils. They told him that Scatha lived on an island. They said he would have to cross to the island by a dangerous bridge, where many a king's son had met his death.

"This bridge is high in the middle," one of them explained, "and low at each end. When you step on to it, it narrows until it is no wider than a hair. Then it squeezes up very tight so that it is no longer than an inch. Finally, it rises right up into the air as tall as a ship's mast."

Three times Cú Chulainn tried to cross the bridge, and three times he was thrown back off it.

The other lads were all laughing at him, and this made him angry. The hero light shone around his head, and he went for the bridge one more time with a great leap into the middle of it. Before the bridge got a chance to change, he leapt over to the other side and landed outside Scatha's house.

Scatha's daughter was sitting at the window doing her embroidery. She looked up and she saw a young man crossing the bridge. She fell instantly in love as soon as she saw his fine handsome face under his thick thatch of curly black hair. Her cheeks flushed bright red, and then the blood drained from her face and she went deathly pale. She looked away from him, and tried to continue with her embroidery, but she

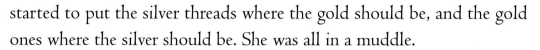

started to put the silver threads where the gold should be, and the gold ones where the silver should be. She was all in a muddle.

Scatha smiled to see her daughter's confusion and asked her if she liked the young man. The daughter replied, "Well, I do, but I am quite sure there is a young girl back in that lad's country who is desperate for him to come home safe to her." Which, as we know, was true. Emer was waiting faithfully at home for Cú Chulainn, ready to marry him.

When Cú Chulainn had crossed the bridge, he went up to the house. It was enormous, with seven tall doors and seven tall windows between each pair of doors. He struck one of the tall wooden doors with his spear, and the spear went right through the door, so powerful was his knock.

Scatha saw how Cú Chulainn was able to pierce the wood of her enormous stout door just by tapping on it with his spear, and she knew she had found a star pupil. She was going to enjoy teaching him.

"You are welcome," she said with a smile.

"Will you teach me?" Cú Chulainn asked.

"Yes," Scatha replied, and she took him on as a pupil and taught him all she knew.

Cú Chulainn spent a year learning weapon skills from Scatha, but just as he was finishing his training, a war broke out between Scatha and Aoife, Queen of Shadows.

Cú Chulainn joined forces with Scatha and her family to defend their

territory. Cú Chulainn and the sons of Scatha killed all the warriors that Aoife sent out to meet them, and in the end, it came down to single combat between Cú Chulainn and Aoife herself.

Aoife was a famously brave warrior, but Cú Chulainn had a plan. Before he went out to fight her, he asked Scatha, "What is the most precious thing in the world to Aoife? What does she care about most?"

"That's easy. Her chariot and horses," Scatha replied.

Aoife and Cú Chulainn fought long and hard, and when the fight was at its height, Cú Chulainn cried out in a loud and alarming voice, "Oh, look! Aoife's chariot and horses have driven over that cliff and are lost!"

Horror-stricken, Aoife turned to look and, while she was distracted, Cú Chulainn threw her to the ground and put his sword to her heart.

"You tricked me," snarled Queen Aoife. "It's not fair. You can't kill me now, having bested me by trickery."

"I don't want to kill you," said Cú Chulainn. "I just want you to make peace with Scatha." He held the blade of his spear against her skin, so she could feel the cold sharpness of the weapon.

Aoife had no choice but to agree, and that was how Cú Chulainn put an end to the war between Scatha and the Queen of Shadows.

Now it was time for Cú Chulainn to go home. He took leave of Scatha's household and set off, back the way he had come.

On his way home, he was walking along a narrow cliff path when he saw an old woman coming towards him. There was no room for them to pass each other, so Cú Chulainn leapt off the path and hung down the cliff face, holding on to the ledge with just his fingers, to leave room for the old woman to pass.

As she went by, instead of thanking him for being so helpful, the old woman stamped hard on his fingers, to make him let go and fall to his death. But Cú Chulainn leapt back up on to the path and cut her head off. It turned out that she was the mother of some of the warriors he had killed in battle, and she had deliberately set out to knock him over the cliff.

After many trials and tribulations, Cú Chulainn arrived back in Ireland, and went to look for Emer. Now, while Cú Chulainn was away, Emer's father had tried to marry her to a chieftain of his choosing. But Emer refused, and so her father locked her up in a castle.

When Cú Chulainn arrived at the castle, he was met by Forgall's warriors. They were three deep around the walls, but Cú Chulainn was now so skilled in the use of weapons that he easily killed them all, one by one, with his sword, and fought his way through to the middle of the castle.

There he found Emer all alone in a tiny room. He swept her up in his arms and put her up in front of him on his horse, and away they sped to Conor Mac Nessa's royal palace.

Great was the feasting and rejoicing at the wedding feast of Cú Chulainn, Ulster's finest warrior, and Emer, his beautiful bride.

 # Labhra with the Horse's Ears

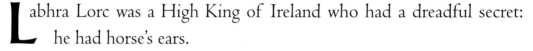

Labhra Lorc was a High King of Ireland who had a dreadful secret: he had horse's ears.

For this reason he always wore a hood, and he never let it down. Even when he wore his golden crown, it went on over his hood. People thought it a little strange, but nobody asked any questions because, after all, he was the king and he could do what he liked.

Like everyone else, Labhra Lorc had hair on his head, and like everyone else's hair, it grew. He would let it get quite long, but once a year, he needed to have it cut.

The problem was that Labhra hated the idea of the barber seeing his shameful horse's ears. So, every time the king had his hair cut, he immediately had the barber killed.

Nobody knew why the king killed all his barbers, but they knew it was not a good thing to be asked to cut the king's hair. So every year, when the king announced that it was time for the royal haircut, the people would draw lots, and whoever 'won' the draw would be sent to cut the king's hair.

Now, one year, the only son of a poor sick widow was chosen to cut the king's hair. The mother was in despair. She went to the king to plead with him for her boy's life.

"My son will be honoured to cut Your Majesty's hair," she began, "but please, please, do not put him to death after he has done it. He is my only child, my only relative in all the world. What will become of me if he is killed? Who will look after me in my old age?"

The king felt sorry for the poor woman, so he agreed that he would not kill the boy. When the young man came to the palace to cut the king's hair, the king spoke seriously to him.

"You are to cut my hair," he announced.

"Yes, sir," said the boy nervously.

"You know what happens to people who cut my hair?"

"I do, sir," said the widow's son. He was shivering in his shoes.

"Well, that is what will happen to you – "

"Yes, sir," said the boy in a tiny voice.

"IF you ever tell anyone my secret," the king finished.

The boy jumped. Had he heard right? He was not to be killed for cutting the king's hair – only if he revealed the king's secret, whatever it might be.

"Do you swear never to tell anyone what you see when you cut my hair?"

The boy's heart was thumping. He could hardly believe it. "Oh, yes, sir!" he cried. "Most certainly, sir."

And so the king lowered his hood, and the young man gasped to see horse's ears sprouting out of the top of the king's head. But he said not a word and he cut the king's hair as carefully as he could.

As he left the palace, the king said, "Mind you never tell a soul what you have seen today."

And the young man promised that he would not. He went skipping home to his mother, glad to be alive.

At first all was well, but as time went by the young man felt more and more burdened by his secret. It felt like a weight inside his chest, and he became quite ill with the worry of it. The doctor was sent for, but he could do nothing for the boy because he did not seem to be really sick.

By and by, a druid came to see the young man, and the druid asked him what had happened. The boy told him the story. He said he had a secret that he had promised never to reveal, and that it was like a weight inside his chest. The druid understood, and he explained that keeping the king's secret, whatever it might be, was killing the young man.

"You will have to find a way to get rid of this dreadful burden," said the druid. And this is what he advised. "Go out to the crossroads and turn right. Tell your secret to the first tree you meet."

The young man did as the druid suggested. The first tree he met after he turned right at the crossroads was a willow. He knelt beside the tree

and whispered into the trunk, "Labhra Lorc has horse's ears."

When he had told his secret to the tree, he felt much better. The weight inside him lifted, and soon he was well again.

One day soon after this, the court harpist's harp got broken, and he needed wood to make another one. So he went outside and selected a fine willow tree. He was not to know, but it was the very willow to which the widow's son had told his secret. The harpist cut down the tree and took the wood home and cut it into pieces of the right size and thickness — and he made a beautiful new harp from it.

The harp was very fine, and the harpist could not wait to play it, but he had promised the king that he would not play a single note on it until the king was present to hear it. So that evening he took the harp to the castle, and all the people gathered around to admire it. And then, at a signal from the king, he began to play the harp.

But when the harpist played on his lovely new harp, instead of letting out sweet harp music, the harp began to speak, and this is what it said. "Labhra Lorc has horse's ears, Labhra Lorc has horse's ears."

All the people were listening, and when they heard this they were astonished, and they started to mutter and shake their heads. "Oh, the poor man," they said to each other. "He is so embarrassed about his ears. What a shame!"

When the king saw that the people did not make fun of him, but felt sorry for him, he realised that there was no need to keep his secret any more. So he took off his hood and revealed his extraordinary ears.

Everyone clapped when they saw the king's ears. They clapped and laughed and said, "What an amazing king we have. Whoever would have guessed it? Horse's ears!"

After that, the king was proud of his ears, and he went about with his hood down and his ears sticking up from under his crown. And never again did the king's barber have to be put to death.

Gaelic Names

It's hard to explain in writing how words sound, so this is just a very rough guide to the way some names are pronounced.

Butterfly Girl

Ailill – A-lill
Etain – Pronounced Eh-tain, with the emphasis on the second part.
Étar – A-tar.
Midir – M'dear

The Enchanted Deer

Fianna – Fee-eh-nna
Fionn Mac Cumhaill – Finn (or Fyunn) McCool
Sadhbh – Sive (rhymes with hive)
Oisín – Usheen

Land Under Wave

Fianna – Fee-eh-nna
Fionn – Finn (or Fyunn)
Diarmaid – Deer-mid
Oisín – Usheen

The Children of Lir

Aoife – Eefa
Fionnuala – Fin-oola
Lake Derravaragh – Derra-var-ah
Lir – Rhymes with 'fir'

The Enchanted Birds

Brú na Bóinne – Broo na Boyna
Dechtire – Dec-tirreh
Lugh – Rhymes with Hugh
Sualtim – Sool-tim

Cú Chulainn and Emer

Aoife – Eefa
Cú Chulainn – Coo-hullen
Emer – Eemer
Forgall – For-gal or Fergal
Scatha – Ska-ha

Labhra with the Horse's Ears

Labhra Lorc – Lowra Lurk